AURORA

BETH BALL

Published by Grove Guardian Press

Edited by The Blue Garret

Cover design by MiblArt

ISBN 978-1-952609-04-6

Hardback ISBN 978-1-952609-05-3

Ebook ISBN 978-1-952609-03-9

groveguardianpress.com

To Momo, Meema, and Connie
For showing me what it means to be thoughtful, caring, and strong

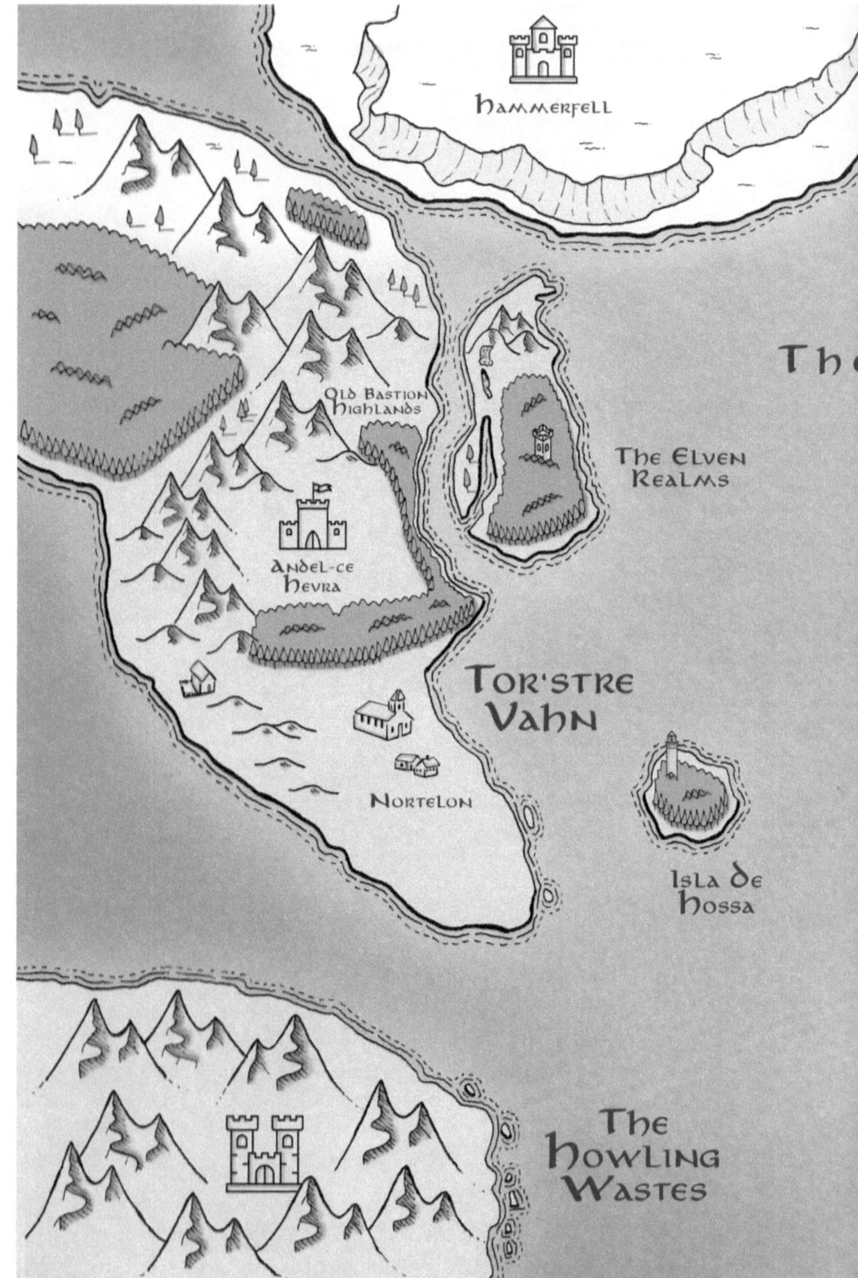

Hammerfell
Old Bastion Highlands
The Elven Realms
Andel-ce Hevra
Tor'stre Vahn
Nortelon
Isla de Hossa
The Howling Wastes
The

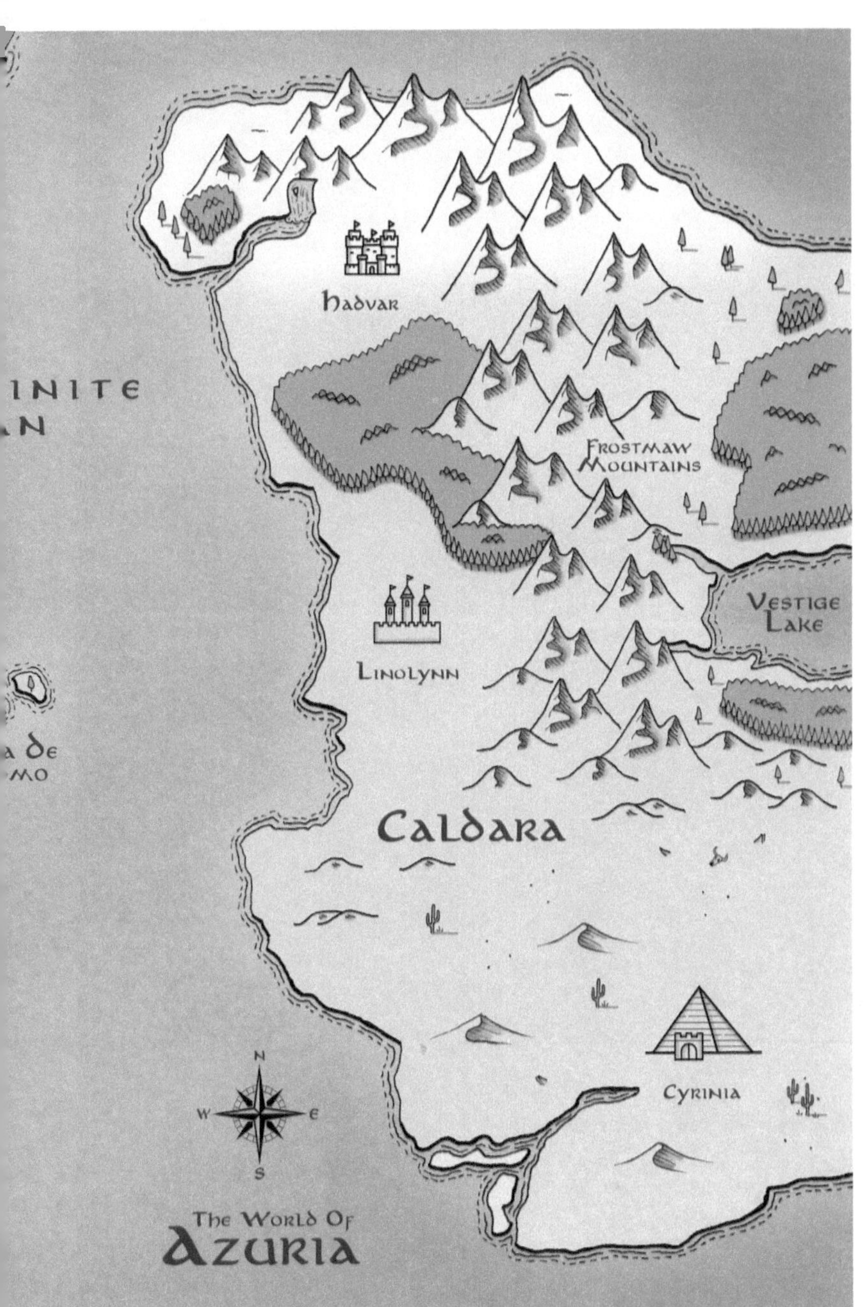
INITE
AN
a de
MO
Hadvar
Frostmaw
Mountains
Vestige
Lake
Linolynn
Caldara
Cyrinia
N
W
E
S
The World Of
Azuria

CHAPTER 1

DORRIC

AURORA ESTATE

"It began at a dance," Dorric would recount for years afterward, "as these stories often do." He and the other elven diplomats had gathered in the courtyard beside the gardens to make their grand entrance. Flowers exhaled sun-warmed pollens, tempting traveling elves and bees with their heady aromas.

Dorric had traveled from Thyles Thamor, a city embedded in the forest, but the mingling of sharp and subtle florals on the sea air brought back memories of Invae Alinor, his childhood home—moments of laughter, of reading by the docks, of gazing out at the sea. Six weeks had passed on the Infinite Ocean, sailing vast expanses of practically uncharted waters toward the sunny shores of Caldara, but they had arrived at last.

Linolynn was a small kingdom, and quite young,

only a century or so older than his own grandparents, but its crown prince had great plans for his city-state's future and aimed to make it a presence felt on the world stage.

Their captain had docked the fine elven craft in the estate's natural harbor, and Prince Arontis himself had greeted the delegation on the dock and ushered them to the estate, its white stone and glass exterior winking brightly at them as the sun tiptoed toward the horizon. Now, feasts, revelry, and new acquaintances awaited them.

The ballroom swirled with color, gemstones flashing as men and women paraded across the dance floor in fine evening dress. A twirl of sapphire and gold swept past Dorric, accompanied by a fragrance that took him a moment to place. Gardenia. The human woman's long, loose curls performed a waltz of their own as she spun across the floor, each tendril of golden hair bouncing in time to the enchanting symphony.

Her partner, an elderly gentleman, was far from her equal as a dancer, yet the two looked happy together. The adagio rose to a crescendo, and the couple drew closer, then apart, bowing with the final chords. Gloved hands patted together, muted applause for the court's musicians. The two parted, and the older man walked away.

Dorric bowed low with a flourish before him. "Dorric Themear, at your service, sir."

The man's bushy eyebrows muted any surprise he might otherwise have expressed at such a blunt introduction, but what were grand balls for if not to meet and be met? "Master Ketch"—he smiled and bowed his head—"though you may of course call me Laurence if you like. No one else does." His eerily pale blue eyes twinkled.

Dorric laughed. "Perhaps Master Ketch would be best then, for the time being."

"Quite so, quite so." Laurence grinned again and gallantly offered Dorric his elbow to show him over to the drinks table. Crystal goblets held sparkling beverages of pale gold, and shades of orange glinted off the glass faces with the deepening light outdoors. "May I ask how you find Linolynn thus far, master elf?"

"Very engaging, sir. In other circumstances, I might add that first impressions of a place can be deceiving, but I have an unshakeable feeling that Linolynn is just as captivating as it has thus far appeared to be."

The laughter of Master Ketch's dance partner bounded toward him from across the finely appointed hall. The marble flooring was inlaid with lapis lazuli, and the ceiling was painted the palest sky blue and gold. The curving white walls and mirrored doors shimmered, and wide terraces opened onto another branch of the estate's gardens, allowing the sea air to drift in and among the guests.

"Pardon me." Dorric shook his head. "It's just that the appointment of this room . . . I have traveled through many human settlements, some as old as Thyles Thamor, others barely settled. It is not often that I have encountered such . . . hmm, is 'modest elegance' the best phrase?"

Laurence nodded, gazing around the room, forehead wrinkled to raise his brows above his drooping lids.

"To speak more directly, sir, I've never been any farther north on this side of the world than Cyrinia, which isn't really north at all. I find it absolutely enchanting." Dorric sighed, turning to take in the movement of the room alongside his new acquaintance.

"Her name is Emelyee. Lady Emelyee Amastacia. Soon to be a duchess."

The sparkling bubbles in Dorric's drink nearly choked him. "Pardon?" He muffled his cough with the cuff of his sleeve.

Laurence chuckled. "The woman you've been staring after. Lady Amastacia, one of the brightest jewels of our court."

"I, um, yes, thank you. She's quite beautiful. My apologies, I mean no disrespect."

"I did not perceive any, my young friend." A teasing grin played out in the man's bright eyes.

Surely he knew of the long-lived nature of the elves? Even if Laurence was one hundred, he would be only half the age of the youngest diplomat present.

Laurence sipped his champagne. "This is her family's estate, you see. Aurora. Though her husband, that man over there"—he indicated a cluster of human men in their late young and early middle years—"has his sights set on expanding their fortunes even further with more profitable properties."

Dorric's heart slumped against the wall and slid to the floor. He bit the inside of his lip. "Her husband, which one did you say he was?"

"Ah, yes, they do look rather alike from here. That one"—he nodded again—"with a slightly yellowing complexion and frown."

The man Laurence indicated had a severe look and calculating eyes. He leaned forward, arguing with his companions. "Thank you, Laurence, I appreciate it. Might I find you again, later in the evening, as I make the rounds?"

"I would appreciate that, Dorric Themear." The elderly man patted Dorric's arm and wandered away to investigate the selection of cheeses.

A pleasant fellow. Had he meant the comment about the soon-to-be duchess as a warning? If so, the intent hadn't been unkind. Any desire of that sort on his part was impractical, traveling as he did. And it would take the council several years to nurture a new diplomat and raise them to even half his level of expertise. The woman, Lady Amastacia, glanced in her husband's direction now and again but, as far as he could tell, those looks were never returned.

Dorric mingled among several of the other nobles and their guests. Each person he met was charming, and they were all easily amazed by any mention or tale of the world beyond their own borders. Did this court not travel?

Each conversation pulled him closer to the beautiful young woman. As Dorric watched, a man with brown hair and a full beard whisked the woman's friend away across the floor, and she was left alone.

Her eyes flashed in his direction, the blue of the

summer sky ringed by the blue of the open sea, and Dorric was at her side.

He bowed deeply and then extended his hand to take hers. "Might I ask you to dance, Lady Amastacia?"

A bright smile, like he was the first to request this honor. Full lips, mauve, and a slight flush against her beige skin. "You may, sir, though I haven't the pleasure of knowing your name as you know mine."

Dorric gently squeezed her proffered hand and led her out onto the dance floor. They joined the group of dancers near her friend. Her long fingers fit perfectly inside his. "Is it not a diplomat's business to learn such things?"

The music began and he pulled her closer, her waist warm through the silk of her gown.

"It very well may be," she said. A closed-lip smile. "And do you claim such motivations for yourself?"

"I do, dear lady, though I could not in good faith promise that my happening upon such knowledge was motivated by duty alone."

Emelyee laughed as she twirled away to another partner, as the dance required.

Dorric took the arm of an older woman with graying hair for their turn about the room. What might Lady Amastacia say in response? Would she be offended? He ought to say something to the woman beside him, or at least inquire her name. He turned to speak, but the chorus resumed. His new partner winked at him as they parted, and Emelyee reappeared. He took her hand once more.

However uncomfortable, he would wait for her to speak. Her eyes evaluated him behind long lashes. Curious, but not disapproving. Likely elves were as foreign to her as they seemed to be to the rest of the court.

Suddenly Emelyee stiffened, her back rigid and hand tensed. Dorric spun her around. Her husband had looked at her at last. Dorric twirled her once more, back to face the opposite end of the ballroom from where her spouse stood in his cluster.

"My name is Dorric Themear, Lady Amastacia."

A slight nod in response. The ease and laughter had left her eyes.

"I understand this is your family's estate?"

She nodded again.

"I am sure you have heard this before, countless times tonight even, but I must say, it's breathtaking. And with its own harbor, a fine location indeed."

Finally, she answered him. "Aurora is a gorgeous estate, Master Themear, I thank you. We are honored to host his majesty's esteemed guests from faraway lands." Her smile didn't reach her eyes.

"Dorric, my lady, is fine." He squeezed her hand. They were back near her friend. "And when you say 'we,' do you speak of the Duke and Duchess Amastacia? I would be delighted to meet your undoubtedly kind and generous parents."

Emelyee shook her head. "I'm afraid they've remained at the castle in Linolynn, Io Keep. The journey is too far for them, and they are not well. My son and his nurse have remained at the capital as well."

"I did not realize you had a son, lady." Dorric sighed. As a younger man, he had dreamt of having children, but after his parents passed, his people were better served by his travels. "How splendid. He must be quite young. May I ask his name?"

"Bruden. He's just turned three."

Her shoulders had relaxed, and the gracefulness of her earlier movements returned. "Wonderful." Dorric smiled at her. "What a lucky young lad. Does he take after you?" He pictured a blue-eyed baby with golden-blonde curls poking out across his scalp.

Emelyee's smile blossomed into a delicate chuckle. "Speaking honestly, no, not greatly." She shook her head, still grinning. "He's a portly baby, and not the most active or curious, despite a wide variety of possible amusements. But overall, he seems happy, as far as one can tell. He does not speak often, either. Only to myself and his nurse."

"Ah, but what beyond happiness can we ask of the very small?"

"That's true." Emelyee frowned. "I would add wellness to happiness."

She had mentioned her parents' ill health. Was that a concern for the child as well? To reassure her on that front would be presumptuous, but it seemed unlikely she would have been asked to host a diplomatic party if her child were gravely ill.

Dorric grumbled inwardly, again unable to find the appropriate words as the song came to a close. This was his profession, knowing what to say and when to say it, in whichever situation he found himself.

He bowed and kissed the back of the lady's gloved hand. "Until next time, Lady Amastacia."

Dorric spent the remainder of the evening among other members of Linolynn's nobility. He took care to dance with each woman of the court, spending several songs with the kindhearted Duchess Doromir, whom he had met during his first dance with Emelyee. One of the stewards, he couldn't recall which, informed him that her husband had passed a few years prior. The gentlemen of Linolynn's court often left her to herself, which seemed unfitting, and so Dorric took it upon himself to see that she had company and entertainment.

Emelyee's friend, Lady Aurelia Adhemar, found him the next morning on his way outside to explore the grounds. "We would be most happy for you to join us," Aurelia said as he offered her his arm. "Emelyee will be down in a moment, and my husband, Frederick, is tending to our son this morning. The lad has been absolutely insistent about visiting the fishpond."

Dorric chuckled. "What a delightful desire, to attend to the fish. Undoubtedly, they deserve callers as much as anyone else. How old is your son?"

"Kind of you to ask. He will turn two this winter."

Emelyee arrived at the foot of the staircase and waved to her friend, picking up her skirts to hurry and join them. "A year and a half younger than Bruden, then?" Dorric said with a glance toward Emelyee.

"Yes, precisely." Aurelia smiled brightly. "You really

couldn't ask for a better tour guide of Aurora." She nodded to Emelyee as she arrived. "I doubt that anyone loves it more or knows it better."

"She's exaggerating," Emelyee said, "but yes, Master Themear, do join us."

"Dorric, please, your ladyship, and while I do not wish to intrude on your morning together, so long as I have your mutual invitation, I would be most honored."

He offered an elbow to Emelyee as well and skipped forward, much to Aurelia's amusement. "Lady Adhemar, I must confess that I am exceedingly curious about your own favorite aspect of your friend's estate. Though you are not as freshly arrived as myself, you do know what it is to look on its beauty with new eyes. Would you lead the first part of our tour?"

Aurelia consented gladly and guided the party out to the terraces and around to the ocean-facing portion of the estate. Beyond the extensive gardens and kept grounds, Aurora was surrounded on three sides by dense forest, and the fourth looked out on fields of wildflowers, atop low cliffs that fell away to the sea. They followed a well-kept gravel trail that wove along the edge of the forest to the beach.

A gray-and-brown stone house emerged from the woods on the right, overlooking a modest pond. "I would never have guessed this was here," Dorric said.

He dropped their arms to approach, running his fingers along the cool, slightly porous surface of the stone. Peering through the fine windows, he could see that the floors were made of large oak beams, and the interior echoed the varying azure shades of the main house, though was more modest in its choice of furnishings. "It suits the estate well, though it feels, if you'll pardon me, Lady Amastacia, more like a home."

Aurelia beamed at her friend and urged her forward.

Emelyee returned a playful look of reproach to Aurelia and came to stand beside Dorric. "It's my favorite part of the property," she said in a soothing alto. From their short meeting the day before, he had remembered her voice being higher in register. "My mother and I spent the summers here while father was at court. We didn't need the grand house for only the two of us, and she preferred the proximity to the sea."

Now that she'd mentioned it, the roll and crash of the ocean further beyond them echoed in this small forest clearing. It had been only a distant whisper at the main estate. "I find the song of the sea very soothing," Dorric replied. "I grew up near the ocean, hearing the tides come in and out, but moved further inland when I was older." He shook his head. He needn't bore these two noblewomen with his tales from the Realms. "Might we see inside then, Lady Amastacia? If that would be possible?"

"It hasn't been tended to in some time." Emelyee bit her lip, looking sideways at Aurelia.

"That won't bother me in the least, though of course my wish is for you to be comfortable in your own home. I hope it will not entirely compromise your opinion of my observations thus far, but I am inclined to see beauty in all I have the fortune to gaze upon. Life is too complex, too varied, to seek out and magnify tiny flaws."

Emelyee smiled at this, opened the door, and

gestured for Dorric to step inside ahead of her. A fine receiving hall with a cast-iron chandelier greeted him. On the left, it opened onto a sitting area and split in two directions beyond, he guessed to a few bedrooms on one side and a kitchen on the other. Above, behind the chandelier, an intricate handrail protected a walkway for the second story and led to row upon row of books.

Dorric spun in a slow circle, taking in the home's dark wooden inner columns and pale blue paint. "I can see why you love it so much. Is the entire second floor a library?"

"It is, yes. Many of the books are out of place at the moment—we took a selection to the main house in anticipation of so many guests arriving."

"Might I see it? I am fond of personal libraries—I have a small collection myself. And I would love to fully picture a young lady of Linolynn in her summer home, surrounded by books and the sounds of the sea."

The color rose in Emelyee's cheeks, and she glanced at the floor. Aurelia wandered past one of the windows outside, humming. "Yes, of course, Dorric, the stairs are just through there." She pointed to the right-hand side of the hallway.

His heart leapt at the sound of his name on her lips. "You've studied Elvish, haven't you?" he asked from halfway up the stairs.

Her eyes widened. "I have, yes. How did you know?"

"The slight trill you caught with the double *r* of my name, Lady Amastacia." He switched to Elvish. "You captured it effortlessly."

She replied in beautiful, hesitant Elvish. "I have spent

many years studying your people's tongue, though I am afraid you overestimate my talents."

"On the contrary, Lady Amastacia"—he switched back to Caldaran—"I am afraid I had not held them in high enough esteem. A failing on my part I hadn't believed possible." He dashed up the stairs without allowing himself to look back at her expression.

CHAPTER 2

RIDEL

CYRINIA

Ridel leaned toward her crystal sphere. Where was the human woman going, moving away from the elf? He was running up the stairs and she . . . The orb's inner light brightened. She had stepped outside the house to speak with her friend, who was standing at the edge of the woods.

"What are you doing?" The one named Emelyee strode over to her friend with the long, chestnut-brown hair.

Aurelia, the friend, narrowed her eyes and tilted her head to the side. "What do you mean?"

"You keep encouraging him." Emelyee's lips narrowed. Her face compressed into a scowl.

"Encouraging a charming diplomat to be kind to my dearest friend by showing curiosity and interest in her and her home? Yes, of course I am."

"Aurelia, I can't." Emelyee shook her head.

Her friend placed her hand on the blonde woman's shoulder. "No one is asking you to do anything except be a gracious host for our kingdom. You've told me before that you wanted to travel."

"Yes, but not like this."

Aurelia sighed. "You have a better chance of getting to know another place by talking to him. It can't do any harm. Are things truly so bad with Calderon that you're this worried when someone is kind to you?"

"Calderon and I are fine."

"Emelyee, how many years have you been saying that?" Aurelia shook her head and led Emelyee back toward the door to the stone house.

"Not everyone can be Frederick, can they?" Emelyee leaned on Aurelia's shoulder as they walked. Which one of the humans was Frederick? So many of them at this gathering, and she was supposed to remember all of their names?

Aurelia smiled broadly at Emelyee's mention of Frederick, whoever he was. Likely her partner, by her reaction. "That is very true." She patted her friend's hand, nodding. "But you deserve to find happiness. And until the king invites us to move to court, you will remain in need of company and companionship. Master Themear cannot take my place, obviously, so you needn't worry about hurting my feelings."

Emelyee laid her hand on the door handle and smiled at her friend. "Very well, but I am only doing this for you."

Aurelia raised an eyebrow and watched Emelyee return inside.

Ridel whispered to her seeing orb to follow. The elf was in the middle of saying something, but she had missed the beginning of the statement.

"Sorry, I didn't hear you," Emelyee called from the lower floor. Her heels clicked on the wooden boards as she crossed the room and rounded the corner to the base of the stairs.

"I was wondering what you were still doing down there?" The elf smiled widely as he leaned over the railing above. "How am I to navigate this wonderful collection without the aid of its curator?"

Emelyee grinned and hurried up the stairs after him.

❧

Ridel took a step back from the seeing orb. The warped reflection of her eyes showed her blinking back at herself. Was that all? Had she missed a crucial event of some sort? After years of service, she had been entrusted with supervising an elven ambassador flirting with a human noblewoman? Surely Lucien had something else in mind for her mission.

She shook her head and strode away, prowling around the edges of the round room. She ran her hand down her smooth lilac arm, tugging at the black off-the-shoulder strap on the opposite side. Why hadn't Lucien simply agreed to her first solution? He was blind to the reality of what stood before them and was overcomplicating his plight unnecessarily.

How could a child result if its parents were dead? Lucien had been convinced that interfering at this stage would be tantamount to a breach in the Concordance and expose their great mistress. Once the child was born, they could take action. She ran her fingers through her dark, evergreen hair, muttering to herself.

He should have contacted her by now. Why keep her waiting?

Trumpets sounded outside, signaling a grand procession through the main thoroughfares of Cyrinia. Ridel threw her head back and stomped out of the inner chamber. She slung the curtains that faced the street closed to strengthen the illusion of being separated from the dissonance of the old city while she worked. The rooms would be stuffier throughout the afternoon, but anyone passing by would assume the third floor of the residence was empty. She smoothed the sides of her garment's corset and held her shoulders back as she reentered the seeing room.

The noise passed, and the well-wishers who had halted their lives to share in the festivities returned to a quieter state, a dull murmuring as the crowd mingled in the shaded streets below.

Black smoke began to churn inside the orb. Finally. She ran over to await Lucien's appearance.

As usual, his yellowed eyes swam forward from the back of his head to fixate on her. "All proceeds according to our predictions?"

Ridel scowled. "You led me to believe I had been stationed here so I would be near enough to intervene if there were a resurgence on their part. You said nothing of observing matchmaking among members of a human court."

"I thought you would be honored by such a task, Ridel." One of the teeth visible through his partially decayed lip disappeared and reemerged as Lucien smiled. "A long-awaited enemy, arrived at last."

She ran her tongue over her doubled canines, disguising her irritation as a moment of reflection instead. "It's a baby. Why must we be so close by? Where could it go that would be beyond our grasp?"

Lucien's eyes flashed. "It is what the baby represents, both to our mistress and to those she seeks to subdue. Should I appoint someone else to the task? Nadya, perhaps?"

"No," Ridel growled. He had suggested another negata deliberately, trying to aggravate her. "I am here, my lord, and honored to do your bidding. We have need of no one else."

Her master bowed his head, a smirk tugging at the corner of his upper lip like it had been hooked in a snare.

The smoke swirled, consuming the image of her master inside the sphere and dispersing it to the edges, returning the crystal to a pale gray glow.

Ridel resumed her pacing. Surely, at some point, the situation would move apace. Alessandra couldn't possibly be interested in the domestic happenings at this estate. She would look in on the scowling nobleman and see if his activity offered any greater promise. Lucien believed that the one they called Calderon held potential as a future ally in their endeavors, wittingly or not. She wasn't yet convinced, but time would tell.

RIDEL MURMURED HER INCANTATION TO THE SMOKY ORB AND searched the estate for Calderon Amastacia. He sat in a dimly lit room in the estate's lower levels with a few other human men and elves, eyeing his companions carefully. Ridel exhaled slowly—they were already testing her patience.

"Where is your beautiful wife this afternoon, Lord Amastacia? Did she not wish to join our special council?"

Calderon brushed the matter to the side with a smirk. "I believe she is entertaining another of your party—Master Themear, if I recall." The man shrugged. "Regardless, I can assure you that matters of business are of little interest to my wife. I try not to bore her with these sorts of things, lest she exaggerate matters and grow concerned."

The elf beside him nodded. "I am certain you know best."

"Let us speak of more engaging subjects," Lord Amastacia said. "You say that you have great holdings in the Realms, particularly along the river?"

"You have a good memory." The elf chuckled. "And you are correct, Calderon, I do. At the border especially. Our city is much farther inland than yours, similar in some ways to your neighboring kingdom—Hadvar, I believe? Any ship wishing to dock in Thyles Thamor must, first, be light, and second, make it beyond my holdings. I'm sure a man like yourself can deduce the certain promise that offers."

The elf leaned closer. "What is more, the best transportation in the city is by water along the canals, and my assets include a fleet of gondolas for such a purpose. Our partnership would mean that you deal solely with the finest of our own society, of course, much as I'm sure you would guarantee to me?"

Calderon raised an eyebrow, considering.

Was this lord's bigotry the means by which Lucien hoped to puppet him?

"I do prefer to keep my own society restricted, though at times I must compromise that preference on behalf of my sovereign." Calderon lowered his voice. "He hasn't the same standard as myself, though I trust he will before long."

"Quite so, quite so," the elf replied. "We haven't the same luxury, as our council, being five members instead of one, are not so easily swayed."

The human lord patted his companion on the knee. "They will come to see in time, Herve, you'll see. Though I do not yet speak for the entirety of our court, be assured that several of the more enlightened of our city-state are relieved to hear of the changes you and your allies seek to bring about in the Realms. There is no need for your own people to be polluted by the pale elves from beneath the surface or to allow those of a wilder heritage into positions of leadership. Your society will soon see the benefit of allowing only the select to rule. That type of precision and determination is precisely what I hope, for both our kingdoms, as they take this bold new step toward more sophisticated international relations."

Herve—ridiculously named—settled back into his chair with a sigh. He wagged a finger at his companion, a gesture that either meant he was cross or he was both pleased and surprised. "I do hope it's as promising as you say, Calderon. The zealots in Invae Alinor have proven difficult, but we've found allies among the better bred of the pale elves who are developing Shade Rest into a city the rest of the Realms needn't be ashamed of. We have faced some resistance with the nature-worshipers in Thyles Thamor and those obsessed with the fae—similar in some respects to your efforts to adapt your own court to Hadvarian traditions, I believe—but we are making strides."

"And you have the benefit of so much more time than we do," Calderon observed.

"Ah, that is kind of you, but I must say, I envy the quick thinking of yourself and your race. So many of the elves are backward looking and obsessed with our heritage, as they call it—always gazing into the mire of the past. If it weren't for leaders like myself, determined to move our society forward, we wouldn't attain in several centuries what you accomplish in a mere decade."

"You flatter me, Herve, and I thank you." Calderon crossed his arms loosely and looked about the room. "Emelyee was difficult to convince at first, but her father saw the promise of our union and believed in my vision for the future of Linolynn. She was persuaded in time, and her family has enjoyed a great increase in their considerable fortune under my management. She may suffer from turns of fancy now and again, but this is to be expected."

"One handles it as best as one can," Herve added. Their conversation turned to the intricacies of trade, and Ridel made her exit.

Perhaps there was a certain promise to using Calderon. Lucien valued determination and cleverness, but the human's understanding of what it meant to be a visionary was sorely lacking. Creatures of all sorts had been pursuing riches through the ages, but their thirst was never sated. The path to power, though, proved much more satisfying, especially when one had an entire world to rule. If she did well enough, perhaps Lucien might place her over this region of Azuria, temporarily called Linolynn. It was picturesque, and she would enjoy life by the sea.

But enough daydreaming. Ridel leaned forward to glare into her onyx-framed mirror. She adjusted her hair to ensure that her horns were covered before she raised her hood. True intrigue awaited her on the Cyrinian streets.

CHAPTER 3

DORRIC

Following a midmorning meal with Laurence on his third day at Aurora, Dorric wandered down one of the sunny corridors on the eastern side of the castle. Emelyee stood alone on a balcony, looking out across the grounds to the rolling tides of the sea. He stopped short, not wishing to disturb her reverie.

"Master Themear," she called, "is that you?"

Dorric spun on his heel and bowed. "Lady Amastacia, a pleasure to see you this morning. Forgive me, I did not wish to intrude."

"I don't mind the company." She smiled and scooted to the side so there was room next to her on the small balcony.

Dorric leaned on the pale gray balustrade; the stone was cold through his linen shirt sleeves. Crisp, salty air flickered across his skin. "I grew up by the ocean," Dorric said after a few moments of comfortable silence. "This beautiful estate of yours brings back many memories of my home."

"I didn't realize Thyles Thamor was so near to the sea. I thought the city was in the middle of the forest, in the heart of the Realms?"

"You are right about that, Lady Amastacia." Dorric shook his head. "Thyles Thamor is a remarkable city, but I was born in Invae Alinor and moved north when it better suited my parents as they aged. I became an ambassador shortly after their passing."

"I'm sorry to hear they have passed." She turned from the sea to look at him.

When was the last time he had spoken to someone about his parents?

They had left the city of their birth in the middle of the night, his father holding the handkerchief his mother used to suppress her sobs. Dorric had returned from his travels to find dangerous changes taking place in their home, a growing stranglehold by the pale religious zealots from the Underland.

He pushed away the memory and sought one more befitting of Aurora's sunshine. "They lived full, beautiful lives. Very few could hope for better. My mother especially was grieved by the move at first, but even she came to cherish Thyles Thamor over time."

"When was the last time that you were in the Realms?"

Dorric grinned. He had been worried she would ask how long it had been since his parents passed. His people operated across timescapes that were difficult for humans to wrap their minds around, especially at first. "I had a month's leave in Thyles Thamor before our journey here, Lady Amastacia. Before that, I spent some time in other grand cities, Andel-ce Hevra most recently, and a few months with a dear friend in Hammerfell."

"I have heard descriptions of the ancient city of Andel-ce Hevra. And Hammerfell is the seat of the dwarves, is it not?" Emelyee's sapphire eyes sparkled. "How exciting!" She sighed and gazed back toward the sea. "I used to wish to travel, in my youth, though I'm afraid I have not been as adventurous as I'd planned to be then."

She sounded so wistful. "Forgive me, Lady Amastacia, but why did you not travel?" What would be holding back a powerful young woman in a noble court?

"Our desires change as we grow older, do they not?" Her face was half-turned toward his.

"Hmm." A flock of gulls took off from the fields, condensing and expanding in their journey out to sea. "I don't know that I could say. In my experience, some desires grow more acute, and we force others to starve."

She shot upright from her casual leaning position, scowling.

Dorric interrupted before she could express her frustration. "Would you care to accompany me on a picnic, Lady Amastacia?"

A flicker of confused surprise crossed her face. "Oh, I—"

"I've no wish to cause hurt feelings, but I must come clean and express my whole truth." He grinned and returned his gaze to the birds. "The enchanting Duchess Doromir has turned down my invitation, saying that she and the princess will be dining together instead, if you can believe it, so I have come to ask you."

Emelyee's stance relaxed as she laughed. "Why, you must be incredibly discouraged by this turn of events."

"I am devastated." Dorric hung his head in mock defeat. It was true that the duchess had refused him, but this was a far more enticing opportunity.

"And the only hope of rejuvenation you might have?" She raised an eyebrow, waiting.

"Is of course to dine with you instead. Unless, I concede, the princess has also requested your presence at her table, in which case I must dine outdoors, bereft of companionship and joy." *Please say yes.*

"These are high stakes indeed, sir. Very well, I accept your request."

Dorric smiled and gave a flourishing bow. "Excellent, fair lady. Then expect a feast."

❦

DORRIC LED EMELYEE THROUGH THE SOUTHERN GARDENS TO A shady spot at the edge of the woods. He spread out a blanket and began unpacking the basket one of the housekeepers had prepared at his direction. "Might I ask you something that's been puzzling me?" Dorric asked as he withdrew a bottle of wine and two glasses. He took Emelyee's hand and guided her onto the blanket.

"You may." Her lips pursed and then spread into a smile.

"Why is it that in Linolynn, men take women's names, as one would in a matriarchy, and yet the society is still primarily run by men?"

Emelyee extended her arms and leaned back, staring

up at the thin white clouds that drifted off the sea. "It would be perfectly acceptable for Linolynn to be run by a queen rather than a king, and it might be possible for a king to select female advisers, though I do not know of one having done so for the past several generations at least. More than anything, I suppose, it has to do with our founding."

"Oh?" Dorric arranged a plate of food for the lady and one for himself. The woman beside him seemed more relaxed than when she was confined inside the walls of her castle, like a weight had been lifted. Perhaps here, she could set aside many of the strictures that undoubtedly governed the life of a noblewoman. "I'm afraid I don't know the story, Lady Amastacia, though I should dearly love to hear it, if you would be so kind."

Emelyee studied him rather than the meandering clouds. "It is a love story."

"I, future duchess, have always found that to be the best kind."

"Mmhm." She returned the oval of her face skyward but glanced at him from the corner of her eye. "There was once a beautiful princess . . ." Emelyee paused as though the clouds might transform and illustrate her story.

Dorric nodded. "A promising beginning, fair lady. Please, continue."

"A beautiful princess who lived at this very estate. Her doting mother and father had settled to the north and were fashioning a castle for themselves and their future subjects around the foundation of an ancient fortress. As much as they appreciated their first home, it was no place to found a kingdom."

The leaves stirred as Emelyee's tale began, the forest lending its voice to hers. "The princess spent most of her time in the woods around the estate, and each evening, she walked through the trees, returning after dark. The area was safe and well protected, so her parents had little fear of something happening to her." Emelyee leaned forward from her reclined position. "But the princess had a secret," she whispered.

Dorric's eyes widened. Emelyee was enjoying the tale almost as much as he.

"If we were to walk a few hours through the woods," she said, "we would find the overgrown remains of what was once a sacred stone courtyard. It was there that the princess would meet her lover, Sylris, each afternoon she was able, and at times, when the two couldn't bear to be apart, in the earliest hours of the morning, when the rest of her household was asleep."

Sylris was an elven name, indicative of one who revered or belonged to the forest. Dorric had never come across an account that claimed an elven heritage for Linolynn.

Emelyee anticipated his question and shook her head. "Her parents knew nothing of their daughter's relationship with the elf. They believed that she simply had a great affinity for the outdoors, as was common for women of noble blood at the time. While their daughter was gallivanting through the forest—they thought, alone—they dedicated themselves to the kingdom's future. As we all know, an essential aspect of kingdom establishment is ensuring proper lineage. The king and queen interviewed a long line of suitors and visited them and their families. Eventually, they settled on one of the young princes of Hadvar, our neighbor to the north."

"And what did the princess think of that?" Dorric asked. Emelyee's voice had an enchanting, hypnotic quality while telling her story. Their present circumstances faded, and he floated out over the world of the tale, watching from above as the folkloric princess fought to determine her own fate.

"There is a side version of the story that is more widely told, especially in the spring," Emelyee said, "where a prince of Hadvar and a prince of Cyrinia fight for the favor of the princess. Some accounts even have her falling madly in love with the dark-haired northern prince—it's meant to explain Linolynn's stronger relationship with Hadvar than with Cyrinia—but truer accounts reveal that her affections lay elsewhere."

"Lady Amastacia,"—Dorric frowned—"why do you say that these are the less true versions? How do you know?"

Emelyee's fingers rippled through the blades of grass bordering their blanket. "I can only tell you the version that my grandmother told to me." She grinned. "My mother's mother, Olivia, had a . . . feisty way of approaching the world. Her objections were similar to your question—with such a social structure, why didn't women wield more power in the kingdom?"

Her tone turned wistful. "I don't know that I could say what she would think of me now." Emelyee blinked quickly and looked away. "She was the one who taught me to take a closer look at the official account of events, to read as widely as I could and not solely what the castle scholars chose for us. 'The women of Linolynn have had enough decided for them,' she would say."

Emelyee's brow contracted as she imitated her grandmother's voice. Her tone was serious, buoyed by an undercurrent of passion and, he sensed, affection.

"'But we have a history all our own,' she would say. 'It's your responsibility to learn it and to live it. In you, the story lives on.'"

Dorric waited to see if she wished to say more. "She sounds like a woman of great wisdom," he added.

Lady Amastacia smiled sadly. "She truly was."

Why had she said her grandmother would be disappointed in her now, or in who she had become? There wasn't an allowance within the rules of decorum that would permit him to inquire, but how many people asked Emelyee the more difficult or personal questions? Was that part of what she was looking for, why she had agreed to this excursion with him? He was reading too much into the situation.

"Please, Emelyee"—his voice was soft, this first time speaking her name—"I'd love to hear more of the story."

"Yes"—she sniffed and sat up straighter—"my apologies. Where were we?"

"The king and queen were choosing suitors for their daughter behind her back."

"Ah," she laughed. "Of course." Her storytelling voice returned, welcoming Dorric back to the lulling embrace of its waves. "The princess was understandably distressed by this news, and she threatened to flee the kingdom forever if her parents would not relent. The various versions differ in this aspect as well. Depending on who is telling the story, her betrothed was already in love with her or was very prideful."

And which was her version of events, or her grandmother's?

Emelyee grinned, anticipating his question again. "I don't know that one precludes the other, but the pridefulness seems rather certain. Whatever the case"—she took a sip of the medium-bodied red wine he'd selected for their meal—"the Hadvarian prince and his soldiers made their way south, past the new castle, to the family's estate. He promised the king and queen to woo their daughter and bring her back with him to the new capital, where they would be wed."

Dorric shoved away thoughts of the similarities between what he had witnessed of Emelyee's unhappiness—trapped in the responsibilities of her role—and the story she was telling of a princess torn between her duty and her forbidden love. The lady was simply being polite and sharing some of Linolynn's folklore, nothing beyond that. Her sapphire eyes pulled him closer. "The fair princess can't have been pleased with this plan," he said, leaning toward Emelyee.

She lowered her voice to continue the story, keeping the princess's confidence across the centuries. "Like any true heroine, the princess had not been idle during this time. She and Sylris planned to run away together, hoping they might find shelter in a community beyond the boundaries of Caldara where no one knew them. But the princess was afraid. She loved her home, the forest and the ocean she'd known all her life. They were part of her, and she feared that if she left, she would surrender a core part of herself."

"An understandable sentiment," Dorric added quickly. His mother had been certain she would never love a place so well as Invae Alinor. She'd mourned for weeks after they were forced to flee.

Emelyee sat back, and her eyes softened, regarding him. "The princess was blessed in her choice of partner in this regard. Sylris also treasured these woods, loving them all the more for bringing him together with his love. On the night the two were to meet and run away together, the elf and his companions transformed the courtyard into a woodland temple so that they might be married before they left, forever binding part of them-selves with the forest they so cherished.

"The princess sneaked out of the castle, moving silently along the forest path. Unbeknownst to her, the prince had commanded his guards to follow her and find out where she went each night. Several days prior, they discovered the lovers and reported the news back to their sovereign. Enraged by this betrayal, the Hadvarian prince ordered that the elf and his companions be killed."

"Had the princess agreed to the betrothal?" Dorric asked, eyes wide. What kind of man would resort imme-diately to such violence?

"Yet another murky area in the stories," Emelyee said. "I like to believe the princess hadn't"—she frowned —"but the time is past that we might know for certain. The prince's commander was a dutiful man. It grieved him to treat the beautiful princess and her beloved so cruelly, and he had begged the prince to reconsider, to speak with her first before executing the attack." Emelyee lowered her head. "The prince refused. He ordered his commander to see it done.

"So on this final night, the commander, torn between his conscience and his ruler, decided to allow the couple a single kindness before they were parted forever. He and his men waited until the princess had greeted her elven lover and the two had exchanged a passionate kiss before they swept into the circle, killing everyone except the princess and the man she loved."

"How horrible," Dorric whispered. If the traditions of these forgotten elves living across the ocean were similar, very few at the ceremony would have been armed save the couple themselves, girded to stride out into the world together and find their fate. The fae of old were said to forego violence on days of wedding celebrations, the couple's loving union inspiring a sense of camaraderie even between longstanding enemies.

Emelyee nodded. "Sylris stood guard in front of the princess. He cried out at the loss of his companions and drove back the soldiers, but he was one against many. The troop surrounded the pair, and the commander faced Sylris, both men with swords in hand. 'I swear on my life no harm will befall her,' the commander said." Emelyee held out one hand and laid the other on her chest, imitating the leader's plea to the elf.

She shook her head, her eyes narrowing as she embodied another role. "'I'll not subject myself to such cruelty,' the princess shouted. She turned her short blade away from the circle of soldiers and toward herself."

Emelyee set her jaw, imitating the princess's determination.

"Sylris and the commander were both grieved by this declaration," she continued, "for they knew that the world would be a darker place without her in it." Emelyee inhaled deeply. "Sylris spun around to face his beloved. He wrapped his fingers around her wrist and begged her to reconsider. Tears poured from his eyes and washed down his face, knowing the burden he was asking her to take on so that she might live."

Dorric blinked back a few tears of his own. Something about this story was deeply personal to the woman beside him. The emotion of it emanated from her, too much to be contained inside a single heart.

Emelyee's voice had grown slightly hoarse. "With the princess's attention fixed on Sylris, the commander seized his opportunity. He stabbed the elf in the back, ripped out his sword, and spun around to restrain the princess." Emelyee sniffled. "Sylris's last vision was the face of his beloved. The only outward sign that he had passed was a flash of pain and confusion before he began to fall away from her toward the earth's embrace."

Emelyee's expression brightened slightly, her lips curling upward. "But she was the only one to see, as they carried her away, the final spark of life in his green eyes and his lips whisper, 'I love you,' before he grew forever still."

Dorric sighed and sat back. He returned her smile. "I wouldn't have taken you as someone fond of sad endings, Emelyee."

She chuckled in reply. "There's a little bit more, and

then you can judge the happiness or sadness of the tale and its teller."

The elf inclined his head. Had she asked, he would have confessed that the storyteller, for all her loveliness, seemed to him much sadder than he would have ever had her be and that, unlike the woman in the story, whose fate was now beyond anyone's aid, he wished he could do something to help her find a new way forward.

"The princess was closely watched in the days that followed. She returned to her parents and their new castle to be married to the Hadvarian prince. Her spirit seemed broken after Sylris's death, and she consented to the union. Early the next year, she gave birth to a beautiful child, named after his father and the forest where they met. Sylvan."

"Her child was half elven, then?" Dorric was relieved his voice didn't quaver as he spoke.

"That he was." Emelyee grinned. "The princess had one final card to play, and it forever changed the fate of her young kingdom. One summer while her husband was away in Hadvar, she had written into law that the family name in Linolynn would pass down the matrilineal line. It's in her honor that Linolynn's noblewomen select a name beginning with a vowel for their eldest daughter."

Dorric sat back, considering. "Such a beautiful tribute to the princess's legacy, in addition to her own commemoration of the influence of matrilineal heritage." He nodded in approval. "Oh, and the princess, what was her name?"

Emelyee surveyed her estate and glanced at the woods behind her. "Aurora."

"The dawn-bringer. Of course." Her self-satisfied smile was infectious. "Lady Amastacia, a final question. The courtyard from the story—is it still there?"

"It is, as far as I know. I haven't been in some time."

Dorric coughed politely to clear his throat. "If you cared to visit it, I would love to accompany you."

"I would like to see it again." Her eyes wandered back over to him. "And I would be quite cross if you didn't come along with me."

FROSTMAW MOUNTAINS

Large eyes and sparkling wings flickered between Yvayne and her book. She squinted and sat back. Why would the faeries be interrupting her work? The four of them chittered at once, tiny mouths appearing on their bark-like skin.

"Slow down, slow down," Yvayne said in Queran, hands raised. Though their voices were high-pitched, they were easy enough to understand when only one faery was speaking, but as more voices joined, their language drifted into cadences of nature, disguised to outsiders to protect the faeries' homes in the Brightlands or beyond. They panted in their excitement, the sound conjuring an invisible brook gently trickling over a rocky bed.

"Trieste, what is it?" She looked to the eldest of the rescued faeries who had taken up residence in her library.

The tiny woodland being flew a little higher, shoulders back to assert her elevated position. "Visitors, outside!" she exclaimed. "One is new and one is not!"

"New and not?" Yvayne scowled. "Speak plainly. Do you know who is here?" She rose and strode out from beneath the library's expanse toward the center of the ancient tree she'd made into her home.

The faeries gasped, wind whistling through trees, and scurried after her stomping footsteps. Yvayne plucked her longbow from its resting place against the central column and slipped her quiver onto her back.

"It's Cassian," Millicent, one of the youngest faeries, cried. "Cassian and a friend."

Curious. She hadn't heard from the saudad leader in years. Why would he show up unannounced outside her home hidden away in the Frostmaw Mountains? "Wait for me here," Yvayne commanded. She ran her fingers along the feathers behind her head, withdrawing the arrow whose tip was covered in poison. Her enemies would be able to sense a powerful spell, even as well-hidden as she was, but other natural impediments weren't as easily tracked.

The midsummer's evening air was crisp due to the altitude as Yvayne stepped outside. The faeries' pet fireflies shimmered low along the ground, searching for the treats the tiny fae had asked her to hide in the low mountain grasses.

"There you are," a familiar baritone called from across the clearing.

Cassian would have known that she lived in the giant oak tree and not one of its ancient neighbors. Yvayne narrowed her eyes. "A fine night for finding friends," she answered, the first half of their code to test the other's identity.

The saudad laughed. "And a verdant evening for vanquishing foes." Cassian stepped out from beneath the trees' branches, his arm around the shoulders of a woman with bronze skin and long, wavy black hair.

Yvayne tucked the arrow back into its quiver and waited, hands open at her sides in a gesture of welcome. The woman with Cassian regarded her dubiously, her lips pursed as she took in Yvayne's long fae ears and the dark gray tattoos that covered her sepia-hued skin.

Moonlight winked off the saudad's wide smile as they approached. He paused a few paces away and bowed deeply. "My love, this is the one I have been telling you about." He rose and gestured to Yvayne. "My friend, I am introducing to you my darling Esmeralda."

The dark-haired woman inclined her head and grinned at Cassian.

"Please, come inside," Yvayne said. Enough had been declared to the wilds where unseen forces had begun to stir.

Yvayne ushered them down her glowing entryway, lit by small orbs of yellow light, and into the primary chamber of her home. Cassian and Esmeralda settled onto moss-covered stumps while Yvayne prepared a kettle for tea. The faeries, ever curious, floated overhead.

"We come with what we believe to be grave news, *Varra*," Cassian began. "My Esmeralda has been having visions, and we have arrived with hopes that you can help her to make sense of them."

"Though I was not born to the saudad people, I have been gifted with their sight," Esmeralda quickly added.

The scent of sage drifted off the couple. Was Esmeralda a druid then, like Yvayne herself, and did that explain why Cassian had brought her here? She set the matter aside for the present. "Very well, Esmeralda, what did you see?"

Yvayne's dreams had been troubled of late. Their enemies moved, she was certain, but the cause was as yet unclear. However, she wanted to hear the young woman's report before mentioning her own concerns.

"A young half-elven woman stands in front of a snow-covered city built on a plateau in the mountains. In the center of her chest, a red light glows. Her dark ruby hair whips about in the cold winds, and all around her, a howling. In the dream, it is clear to me that she is in danger, but I am unable to act, to warn her. She stands alone, staring at the city, as the shadows around her grow." Esmeralda shuddered and looked down into her teacup.

"What is it?" Yvayne leaned forward. The red glow, it could be—

"She has awoken screaming from the dream each night for the past three nights, Varra," Cassian said. "I thought it was time she came to see you."

"Esmeralda, is there anything more? The glow, or the shadows?" These signs had occurred before.

The young woman ran her fingers through her hair. "These last few nights, the girl, she is . . ." Esmeralda sniffed and wrapped her arms around her waist. "At the end of the dream, she is consumed by the terrible shadows. A gaping mouth appears in the silhouette and engulfs her. She screams."

"Hmm." Yvayne stood and began to pace, asking Esmeralda clarifying questions and carefully pursuing each detail. The snowy city in the mountains was likely Hadvar, the kingdom a few days northwest of her home, but if the young woman was staring at the city, from outside it, she had to be elsewhere.

"There is something else, Yvayne," Esmeralda said. "It is not only in my dreams but in the cards as well. These last four days, my readings are the same." The woman drew a worn deck of violet-backed cards from her satchel, shuffled through them three times, and began to lay them out, sifting through with her left hand to select each one with her eyes closed. She laid three in a line, then one on top, and one below.

The earthen floor hummed with life, natural energy coursing toward Esmeralda. Yvayne inhaled deeply as waves of rosemary wafted toward her, twirling through the sage. "In my readings," Esmeralda explained, "I ask the spirits first to show me where I am, second, where I should go next, and third, what lies further ahead." She overturned the first card, THE HIGH PRIESTESS. "Myself, a figure seeking to expand her wisdom." The second read THE HERMIT. Eerily, a sepia-skinned woman with an antlered headdress stared back at Yvayne from inside a circle of ancient trees, a single light glowing beside her head. The woman held out her hand, beckoning the viewer closer.

Cassian cleared his throat. "In this particular circumstance, we thought this might symbolize you." His dark brown eyes flashed as he grinned at her.

Yvayne raised an eyebrow. Even amid heightened danger, Cassian found the humor in his circumstances. "I understand why you might associate this image with me. I am pleased you came here."

The bright smile glowed against the dark stubble that grew along his cheeks.

"Esmeralda, do continue," Yvayne said.

Her hands shook as she reached for the third card. THE MAGICIAN.

Like the woman Esmeralda had described from her dream, the figure on the card had flowing red hair, and Yvayne had only seen eyes of such intense green a few times in her long life. Plants flared to life beneath the woman's feet, and the six elements glowed in orbs around her. Further back, a pack of wolves howled before a silhouetted forest. "This card says much, does it not?" Yvayne asked.

"It does." Esmeralda's voice faltered. "She is one who brings forth what is unseen. She makes it real. But the remaining two complicate this reading." Esmeralda flipped over the top card, THE MOON, and the lower card, THE TOWER. "Whenever I continue this reading, other patterns emerge across a variety of paths, each branching from this foundation." The woman's hazel eyes burned. "Please, Yvayne, have you an idea of what this means? Can you guide me?"

"I think it is you who is guiding me, Esmeralda," Yvayne said softly. "The tower . . . it signals great change, does it not?"

She nodded. "Followers of Cassandra at times debate whether or not this earth-shattering change can be a positive sign as well as a dark omen, but—"

"What is it that you believe?" Yvayne interrupted her. The saudad had taught her long ago that a fortune's choice of vessel was just as important to pursuing understanding as the fortune itself.

"I believe it is deliberately ambiguous, especially at this rooted position in the fortune. However else the rest unfolds, whichever fate emerges, great change must occur. It is inevitable."

CHAPTER 5

DORRIC

Evening rain lent its cadence to Dorric's thoughts of Emelyee. He imagined petals falling from the flowering trees of Aurora, coating the ground in a pattern unique to this rainstorm alone. The next morning, as the sun emerged and dried them, servants would come and sweep them to the side. Others would crush them beneath their feet. They would brown and join the earth once more. Why did she allow herself to remain so unhappy?

Her delightful presence inspired him toward a better version of himself, a Dorric who was braver, more forthcoming. It was only right, he resolved, that he attempt, for Emelyee's sake, to bring that better elf into being. The next time he saw her, he would speak honestly. *I should dearly love to see you enjoying the*—no, that wouldn't do. *Dearest Emelyee . . .* Was there a way to address the issue that wasn't brash? Or was he simply presuming to know what was best for her, as he sensed Calderon did? Why besides his own feelings should he assume that he knew better?

These doubts clouded Dorric's mind the next morning as he and Lady Amastacia met for their walk deeper into the woods. He was determined to let her speak as she chose and to give her a reprieve from the expectations placed on her by her life inside the court. Anything further would be advancing his own agenda rather than responding to her needs and desires.

Emelyee was quiet on their walk to the forest edges, her mood perhaps dampened by his. They walked through the trees, following a faint path that wound its way through the woodland. The trail narrowed, and Emelyee stepped ahead of him, reaching back to take his hand in hers. Dorric's heart thrummed in his chest, sonorous enough to scare away any creature that prowled nearby. She asked for more details about his childhood, what life had been like in Invae Alinor, the white marble city sheltered entirely by the cave from which it was carved.

Dorric diverted her next set of questions about his travels to ask after her experiences. What had it been like to be a young noblewoman in Linolynn? Where had she visited across Caldara, and where else in the world would she go if given the chance?

After some encouragement, Emelyee detailed her life in Io Keep and her favorite aspects of Linolynn's culture. She had a great curiosity for the future direction of her nation under the prince once he was crowned king.

"From what you told me yesterday," Dorric said,

"your family's heritage connects to this estate, does it not?"

"Yes, Aurora has been part of the Amastacia holdings since before Linolynn was a kingdom." Emelyee glanced back at him.

"If I may be so bold, then, why is it that we have a King and Prince Arontis and not a Queen Amastacia?"

Emelyee laughed heartily, shaking her head. "That wouldn't do at all, Dorric. My mother was not in the line of succession and, besides, she would not have enjoyed being queen. She only has so much patience for dealing with outside matters, and our new princess is far better suited to supporting the throne and managing the court than she or I would be."

Dorric smiled, enjoying her amusement. He raised an eyebrow. "Ah, but I am speaking of you and your mother running the kingdom and having others who would support your rule. That's not treason to suggest, is it?" He spun around, dramatically scanning the woods behind them for Arontis soldiers.

She laughed again. "No, though it may have been under the first King Arontis, more than a century ago." She held up a finger in false caution to him. "Still during your lifetime, as not all of us are as old as you."

Dorric clasped his hand to his chest and gasped, affecting offense. "Your banter wounds me deeply, your ladyship," he proclaimed, "but I shall persevere in spite of this effrontery." He straightened. "You should know that I am still considered quite young for an elf. Why, I have been a diplomat for only sixty-one years! I am in my prime, you see."

"But of course." Emelyee curtsied as much as she was able on the forest path without snagging her dress. "I should never have asserted anything to the contrary." She grinned as she rose. "And to answer your earlier question, through a series of marriages and successions that I was obligated to learn at one time but have since forgotten, the rule of Linolynn passed out of the Amastacia line relatively peacefully. We have retained this estate and are the second most prominent family of the realm."

"How fortunate for the realm," Dorric observed. "I remain curious, Lady Amastacia, what is your life like now?"

Their playful discourse had given him enough encouragement to ask, and he had fulfilled his promise to himself. If Emelyee said that she was happy in her present situation, despite whatever evidence to the contrary, he would press no further. He couldn't wish for her to say that she was dissatisfied either, but a small part of him hoped that she might desire something more.

Her smile faded, and Emelyee grew quiet. She began walking again, without taking his hand, and Dorric followed after her.

After a few minutes of silence, Emelyee told him about some of her daily tasks and her part in the running of a prominent household. She said nothing of Calderon or her son, Bruden. Try as he might, the elf could not silence his inner romantic, who dearly wished to add meaning to this omission.

❦

DORRIC INHALED SHARPLY AS THE COURTYARD UNFOLDED before him. The ancient holy site was perfectly situated at the crest of a rise so that a visitor wouldn't perceive it until just before they arrived. Even then, they would only glimpse enough to enflame their curiosity. He took Emelyee's hand again, gazing at the moss-covered stones.

Below them rested a circular lower level made of planed stone with a few crumbled square platforms that rose out of the ground on either side. The seams between the stones were full of dense, dark green moss that contrasted with the lighter mosses and brilliant green leaves of the surrounding foliage.

The courtyard's upper level created a half-circle around the first, with stairs leading down on either side. From his and Emelyee's position overlooking the courtyard, he could not see where another entrance might have been, the one used by Sylris and his companions in her story, but the layout indicated that the forest had once held a second timeworn path that led either to the opposite end of the mezzanine or perhaps opened onto the lower story. A stone railing, each piece at one time perfectly cut and placed together, remained mostly intact, with only a few of the arches having fallen to the unworkings of time.

At the center of the mezzanine, and likely the focal point of the entire structure, were four stone pillars rising a story and a half high, supporting a domed roof large enough for two people and a cleric to easily fit beneath it and proclaim their love to those gathered below. This must be what Emelyee had referred to when she described Sylris transforming the area into a temple for his marriage to Aurora.

Dorric imagined the elf's first encounter with Aurora, walking through the forest with his friends, or perhaps wandering alone, following his feet to a familiar favorite space from an earlier adventure. In his heart, he would have sensed an imminent shift, a quickening of his spirit, the unmistakable impression that his life would soon change forever. Dorric had felt those same stirrings as he watched the Caldaran coast coming into view.

Sylris's footsteps would have stopped the moment he saw Aurora, unaware that she was waiting for him but drawn by a similar sense of fate. She would have been leaning against the railing of the upper mezzanine, or on the central dais under the circular stone archway. To the young princess, from her position on the terrace, gazing out across the courtyard with its mossy stones holding the secrets of ages past, it would have seemed as though the entire space belonged to her, had been created for her, perhaps precisely for this moment.

The elf would have experienced the great joy and wonder of something known being made new once more.

"Beautiful lady," the Sylris of his imagination called out, wishing to dazzle the young woman without startling her from her reverie, "might I have your permission to trespass on your domain?"

What Aurora would have thought as this transpired, he couldn't say. Maybe these wise human women found elven bravado to be disingenuous, an empty show that aimed to impress those of shorter life spans but quicker discernment. Maybe the princess had only found Sylris interesting because he was different from those she encountered at her estate, though it would have been more common in the past millennia for the Caldaran elves to interact with their human neighbors than it was at present.

Dorric shut his eyes tightly to remove himself from the fantasy of the past and rejoin Emelyee in the courtyard. She had stopped a few paces away from the entrance and leaned against the railing that curved around the lower circle of stones. This was not precisely the positioning he had envisioned for Aurora in Linolynn's past, but it was captivating nonetheless.

It was only as he drew closer to her that he saw the tears gathering in her eyes. "Emelyee," he whispered.

She looked away.

He waited once more, half an arm's length from her, every muscle in his body strained into stillness. An eternal moment passed, and she turned back to him.

Her lower lip trembled, but words did not emerge. She reached out and laid her hand on his chest.

Dorric's jaw clenched, watching her. He tucked his fingers beneath hers and raised them to his mouth, kissing the knuckles.

A tear fell, and still she said nothing. Dorric took a step nearer. His heart leapt as she closed the distance between them. Unable to prevent himself, Dorric ran his thumb over her cheek to wipe away the tear.

Emelyee caught his hand and held it against her face, closing her sapphire eyes.

The sound of his shallow breaths filled the courtyard.

When she looked at him again, her gaze swept between his peridot eyes and wide elven mouth. Dorric needed no other sign. He wrapped his arm around her waist and lowered his lips to hers.

CHAPTER 6

RIDEL

"You're certain you've seen it," Lucien hissed.

"Yes, my lord." Ridel's eyes flashed. "The elf carries the amulet with him during his trysts with the human woman. Your instincts were correct."

"I'm pleased to hear it. You are to be commended." Her master grinned. "Is it finished? Are you ready to proceed?"

Ridel sighed. The two lovers had met often over the past week, usually in the elf's rooms, at times in the stone house by the ocean, and they spent the evenings together exploring the estate's grounds. She would never admit as much to Lucien, but she far preferred observing the two of them, nude and intertwined, than the negotiations between the other humans and the elves. Dorric was passionate and generous with Emelyee, as many of Ridel's own past consorts had been.

"Ridel," Lucien snapped.

"Apologies, my lord." Ridel straightened her shoulders, chastising herself for becoming distracted.

Lucien's upper lip curled in a snarl, but he said nothing.

"It is possible they will need more time to conceive, but I shouldn't think it will take very much longer."

"Very well. Be prepared to warn the husband as soon as may be. Alessandra would prefer the diplomatic negotiations to fall through."

"As you wish, my lord." Ridel bowed her head until she was sure Lucien had vacated the orb, not wanting him to witness her eagerness to move forward. By her calculations, the human woman should be near her time if not already past it, and she wanted to prepare a special torment to pay Calderon back for the meetings he'd forced her to endure. The Cyrinian spice market offered much in this regard. The desert people had long been students of magically induced dreams.

RIDEL STOLE THROUGH THE LANTERN-LIT STREETS OF THE Cyrinian market, searching for the mulberry awning trimmed with gold that had caught her eye before. There, behind the empty fruit stall. She secured her hood before slipping between the carts and down the alley. Ridel fiddled with her metal pins for a few moments until the lock clicked free, and she darted inside.

Beams of moonlight cast their glow against stacks of bags and crates in the storage room. Ridel picked her way through carefully. She murmured a spell to silence the owner's beaded curtain and stepped into the store proper. Packages of tea and exotic spices swirled through her senses. How many deadly poisons waited to emerge from among so many seemingly innocent ingredients? They only needed an expert hand to set them free.

Pppst. An orange light fizzled into existence. The shopkeeper held a long match to a hanging lantern and bathed the shop in soft yellow light. "I heard you come in," the woman's husky voice said. Dark purple eyes glittered against golden skin as she smiled. "And I know what you're looking for."

Ridel slowly slipped the dagger she kept sheathed against her left thigh free. "That's very convenient, thank you." She dropped her voice an octave and disguised her accent, cleansing it of any regional markers that might indicate the northern reaches of Caldara.

The woman stepped between the barrels placed at intervals around her shop and peered at a thin row of shelves containing variously sized potion bottles. "You wish to influence dreams, do you not?"

Ridel inhaled sharply. How had she known? The piles and concoctions spread around the shop amid herbs and spices disrupted Ridel's energetic reading of the woman in front of her. "I see that you are a practitioner of the arts you enable for others." She spoke slowly, luring the shopkeeper into a sense of ease.

The golden-skinned woman chuckled. "Surely this cannot be a surprise, can it?"

A hint of ash clung to the air, burnt sage and—Ridel sniffed again—birch, perhaps. "No, indeed, you misunderstand me. I am pleased your expertise is as extensive as I've been told." Flattery rarely harmed tense situations. Ridel's fingers grazed the cool hilt of her dagger, ready at a moment's notice.

"Ah, here we are." The shopkeeper plucked a spherical vial from the crowded shelves. "For full potency, rest this mixture on a bed of hawthorn beneath the light of a full moon."

These fortune-tellers and herbalists were all the same, placing their faith in outdated rituals that harkened back to a long-dead age. But Ridel didn't need such extravagances to cast her spells. "Where is one to find hawthorn in the desert?" She could at least pretend to plan on performing the ritual.

"By your left hand." The shopkeeper smiled. "Will there be anything else?"

What she wouldn't give for powdered satyr hoof. A tiny pinch blown in the face of one's enemy and *poof*—instant unconsciousness. If this woman were older—Ridel squinted at her—she might have some of the useful old concoctions, but even if her heritage was as elven as it appeared, she couldn't be more than a few hundred years old.

Ridel sighed and held out her hand for the vial. "No, this will do perfectly, thank you."

"*Bena lorçane,*" the shopkeeper said, her hand raised with palm facing out as she bowed, a wish for a powerful enchantment.

Ridel grinned in reply and slipped back through the beaded curtain and out into the slate-gray streets of Cyrinia. Perhaps the shopkeeper kept a stash of more exotic ingredients in the cellar? She eased her hood over her horns, smirking at the lantern lights. The city hadn't failed her yet with its store of surprises and diversions.

❧

YVAYNE

Yvayne gestured for Cassian and Esmeralda to enter silently so as not to disturb Lita's report. "You're certain she didn't leave with anything else?"

"I am." The gold-skinned elf nodded, her eyes widening when she perceived the other two on the edges of the seeing circle.

"It's alright, they're part of how I knew to contact you in the first place."

Lita bowed her head to the two saudad.

"She has the gift as well," Yvayne said, indicating Esmeralda.

"I do, yes." Esmeralda stepped forward. "Cassandra smiles upon me."

The elf grinned. Unlike the saudad, they did not credit single deities with such gifts, though Lita would never fault another for doing so. "I am glad you have aid both far and near."

"As am I," Yvayne answered. "You will tell me when she leaves the city?"

"Yes, Varra, I swear." The herbalist placed her palms together and bowed her head.

Yvayne blew over the bowl, disrupting the vision.

"Was it as you believed?" Esmeralda asked. "They will target the girl?"

"So it seems." Yvayne bit her lip. Had they missed something in their fervor to see the child brought into the world? Was it still before her time? "Lucien will wait until she is older to mount an attack of his own. But Alessandra, she does not enjoy games in the same way her servant does." Yvayne wrapped her arms tighter around herself. *Think.*

From what they had observed, Lucien bore little affection for Ridel and would likely dispose of her after she completed her task. His methods had changed little through the ages. Alessandra was aware of this, too, and might twist the negata servant to her own ends.

"Varra"—Caasian's baritone interrupted her thoughts—"there is one other reason why we've come."

Yvayne looked between the two of them in confusion.

"I fell into a trance of sorts, following the third time Cassandra laid the same cards out before me." Esmeralda held out a small wooden figure on the palm of her hand.

Yvayne took the figure from Esmeralda and lifted it into the light. The carving matched the width of her palm. Esmeralda had made it from a rowan tree and shaped the wood into the figure of a dryad, caught midway between her transformation from a tree to a feminine form. One arm stretched overhead, and her head tilted back, half branches, half hair. A woven strand bearing three small raven's feathers dangled from the delicate, barely emerged ankle.

"Something told me you might need it," Esmeralda said. She bit her lip, waiting on Yvayne's reaction.

The druid traced the feathers that hung down from

her braids. "I love it," Yvayne said, her voice low. "It's more perfect than I can say."

RIDEL

Ridel winced as she drew the curved blade through the flesh of her hand. Her skin screamed as she squeezed her fingernails against the edge of the cut, swirling the black liquid into the bowl she'd placed beneath the orb. She smirked. Magic ran in her blood. The negata had no need of superstitious herbs or the light of the moon. They carried fire within.

"Calderon Amastacia," she whispered over the metallic liquid. The streams of blood took on dark, shadowy shapes as they swirled, searching for the soul she had named.

The young lord tossed in his sleep, his mind clearly already disturbed. Ridel's eyes sparkled. She could make even better use of that. The dream she brought him out from was less than intriguing. He ran through the streets of a nondescript town, dirty, fleeing from—

Ridel began her revisions. His feet flapped against hard cobblestones as he hurried to confirm what he had long suspected. *Yes,* she encouraged his subconscious, *you have known what you wish to deny . . .*

Assuring humans that they had anticipated the disasters that befell them made them more pliable in their reactions.

"Your true blindness is lifted," Ridel whispered.

Her subject froze, turning about.

She blew over the water, casting him into complete darkness.

He ran forward.

Ridel slowly lifted the light and sent him tumbling through the halls of his castle, searching down endless corridors for his wife. His dream self happened upon Emelyee and Dorric in an elegant library, whispering together on a dark green settee.

"We have amazing schools in the Realms," Dorric urged. Best to let Calderon believe he would be losing two family members instead of only one. "There will be much for Bruden to learn." The elf ran his hand along Emelyee's thigh. Calderon's protest reverberated through Ridel's rooms. *Good.*

She pushed the dream forward, showing the human a taste of what she had witnessed unfolding between the two lovers. "Right under your nose, and a foreigner," she whispered, leaning into his fear and hatred of nonhuman peoples. "Soon you'll lose everything that once belonged to you."

Calderon screamed in rage.

Though she held his body frozen in the dream, his mind turned immediately to violence. *Very good, my pet. Very good.*

"You know what to do," Ridel hissed. "You were right not to trust them."

She blew darkness back over the dream as she left. With a single stroke, she had endangered the child's future and disrupted the elven delegation. The first step toward exchanging Lucien's rule for the dark goddess Alessandra herself.

CHAPTER 7

DORRIC

An evil presence pulled Dorric from his sleep. Something dark moved in the ancient castle. A chilly draft blew in from his cracked window. He wrapped his cloak around himself and stepped out into the white marble halls. Perhaps Emelyee had sensed something too and would come and find him.

They usually met for a light breakfast before a walk together, or they would pay a visit to the Adhemars in their rooms. He had grown quite fond of the grinning baby, a lad named Teodric.

Dorric began to pace the library stacks. The sun rose. The air warmed. And still no Emelyee.

He sprang forward when the library doors opened at midmorning.

"Dorric, is that you?" Laurence peered into the library shadows, searching for him.

"I am here, Master Ketch." Had the elderly gentleman come with a message from Emelyee? Dorric's heart froze at the sadness on his friend's face. "What is it? Is she alright?"

Laurence sighed and sank slowly onto one of the leather sofas. "I am afraid that certain events have come to light, my young friend."

"You still haven't said—"

"Lady Amastacia is well enough, Master Themear, though I think it may be best for you to seek the safety of your own ship."

Dorric squeezed the back of one of the plush chairs. "Laurence, you don't understand. She's leaving with me. We've . . ."

Laurence shook his head. "I do not think the lady will be departing for the Realms, Master Dorric. She is not an explorer like you."

"I have to see her." Dorric straightened his waistcoat and smoothed back his auburn hair. They would talk this over, he would assure Emelyee of his love for her, and she could make her decision.

Her words from the day before came floating back to him. "I cannot give you what you want, Dorric. I don't have it."

"You mistake me, my love," he had said. "It is I who wish to give to you. Allow me a chance, let me try. I won't ask you for more."

She sighed, her sapphire-blue eyes blazing back at him. "You already have."

"There's more you must know." Laurence pulled him back to the present. "Lord Amastacia has called off the diplomatic endeavors. All of the elves have been asked to leave."

"What!" After all of the work everyone had expended, the relationships formed—

"He is a jealous man, Dorric, and powerful. Even in your extensive travels, you'll have met few so determined to have their way." Laurence shook his head. "You returned light to one of the bright stars of our court. But that will need to be enough. Please, let me walk you to your ship."

Dorric clamped the sides of his face and threw his head back. "Laurence, I cannot. I must see her." He threw his arms down at his side, resolved. He would try once more.

"Please, as your friend—"

Dorric silenced the old man's pleas with a single look, his own eyes burning into those of his friend. "I will never forgive myself if I don't. Elven lives are too long to be tainted by regret."

"Be cautious, then." Laurence clutched his wooden staff and bowed his head as Dorric left.

Emelyee wouldn't allow herself to stay here, not now. She couldn't reject happiness for a veil of security. His breaths came quickly as he rushed through the halls toward her rooms. She should be free to decide her own fate, whatever the risk to himself.

❧

"You really won't come with me?" Dorric took a shuddering breath.

"No, I can't." Emelyee stood across the room from him, arms crossed around her waist. Her face was contorted by pain, but he didn't dare cross the room to stand beside her. "My place is here."

She spoke as though the words came from someone else. "Your place? Emelyee, that is not how the world has to work. You can go wherever you choose."

"No, Dorric." She shook her head. "This is not a romance or fantasy. There are rules and limitations. I belong here."

"You belong where you would like to be. To have the life that you want."

She closed her eyes, hugging herself tighter. "No."

"Dorric," Reece, Emelyee's guard, called from the door.

"One moment more," Dorric answered. He had only seconds to convince her. Reece had made him promise that he would leave before Calderon's guards arrived.

"Please come away with me." Tears flooded his eyes. What would her life be like if she stayed? The keep she had described in the capital, enclosed on all sides, able only to look out over the freedom of the water. "Please." His voice broke. He wanted so much more for her, but she was afraid. Calderon's manipulations had forced her to retreat into a tiny corner of herself, and she had shut herself inside that prison once more. How could the true Emelyee survive?

She wouldn't meet his gaze.

"Dorric!" Reece pounded on the door. They had waited too long.

The suite's entry doors slammed open down the hall. Dorric rushed across the room to Emelyee and wiped a tear from her cheek. What had she endured that morning already?

Her lip trembled as she looked up at him. Only the slightest flicker of the fire he had seen remained. Resignation had won.

Rows of heavy boots stomped down the hall.

"Step aside," one of the guards commanded Reece.

Emelyee gripped Dorric's hand.

"I follow the lady's commands, not yours."

Two sharp blows, followed by a thud as Reece's body crumpled to the floor.

She gasped and squeezed his hand tighter.

"Emelyee," Dorric whispered.

The door to her room flew open, and two rows of guards draped in the Amastacia black and silver filed inside. The six of them formed a semicircle around Dorric.

He turned away from them and back to her.

Before he could speak, they seized him and pinned his arms behind his back. Unsatisfied with his reaction, the one nearest Emelyee wrenched Dorric's arm tighter.

Dorric groaned as his wrist cracked.

"Wait," Emelyee cried, hands held out toward the guards. They loosened their hold slightly but showed no sign of obeying her otherwise.

Could this be? Was she going to leave with him? Dorric's heart bounded against the base of his throat.

Emelyee's eyes flashed at the guards. "Do as I say." She threw her head back, drawing herself up to her full height.

The two men released him and took a small step back.

Emelyee eyed them coolly and closed the space between herself and Dorric. *Say you're coming with me.*

"We must say good-bye," Emelyee choked out. She pulled her lips between her teeth.

Dorric shook his head. "You can still come with me."

"No," she said again.

Dorric's last shards of hope shattered. He sniffed, clinging to this final moment before he drifted out to sea. "Then take this, my Aurora." He dug the beautiful wooden box containing his mother's amulet out of his pocket. He had no other token of his love that he could leave with her. "You will forever be in my thoughts. And if ever you need me, I will find my way back to you. No matter what."

He wrapped her fingers around the amulet he had inherited from his mother, the symbol of betrothal passed from one generation of Themears to the next. It was forged long ago, she had told him, by an elven woman searching for her true love who had been taken from her. The amulet was born out of her desperation and her hope to find him. It carried love across the ages.

Emelyee closed the amulet in her hand.

A tear fell down Dorric's cheek. He had planned to give it to her when they could return to the courtyard. It now represented an ending rather than the beginning he had hoped for. Dorric stared into her eyes. He had nothing more to tell her.

The guards dragged him away to be borne back across the sea.

Emelyee wasn't permitted a moment alone as they prepared for their return to Io Keep. Calderon glowered by her side as she said her good-byes to Aurelia and Frederick. "I'll explain when I can," she whispered in Aurelia's ear as they embraced.

Frederick peered at her in concern. He stood back away from Emelyee and Calderon, holding his son Teodric's hand. The little boy looked around the courtyard, tiny brow furrowed in confusion. Emelyee guessed he was searching for Dorric, whom he'd developed an immediate fondness for.

Emelyee clasped her friend's hands in hers as they parted. "I will do all I can to help you find a place at court as soon as may be." She squeezed Aurelia's fingers. *I don't know what I shall do without you.*

Aurelia blinked away tears. "I know you will. Our home is always open to you should you need it." Her sea-gray eyes flickered over to Calderon and narrowed. Though she would never say it, Emelyee knew Aurelia thought she'd made a mistake, but she couldn't bring herself to leave Linolynn or her son.

"Take good care, Lady Amastacia," Frederick said, laying a hand on his wife's shoulder. "We'll be alright. Forestvale is beautiful this time of year."

Emelyee gave him a quick smile and blinked to clear her eyes before she turned back to Calderon. He had never understood her friendship with Aurelia, finding even the minor nobles beneath her family's notice. She met his gaze briefly before their steward handed her into the carriage and Calderon climbed in after her. It would be a quiet, tense ride back to the castle.

As the countryside streamed past outside the window of her coach, Emelyee's mind wandered to her stolen moments with Dorric. Her pulse quickened at the memory of his fingertips caressing her neck, the press of his lips and tongue against her skin. The man across from her cared for her, certainly, but she was more of an achievement to him than a passionate partner. This truth sank into the depths of her stomach. That part of her life was lived. She wouldn't repeat it again.

Emelyee ran her fingers over the intricate wooden box that held Dorric's amulet, tracing the grain of the wood and its patterned carving. What did he think of her, following their separation? Would his mind turn to her now and again as the years passed, his life span extended so far beyond hers?

The one thing she asked of Calderon on their drive was that he allow her to tell her parents. Her mother burst into tears immediately and locked herself away.

Her father refused to speak to her, barely looking at her whenever she was in the room.

Emelyee fell ill. At first, she thought her parents' and husband's treatment of her caused her sickness—their prolonged disappointment, punishing her for threatening the lifestyle and rank they held so dear. The truth set in early one morning. She was expecting a child.

She had a few days before anyone else would know, though the maids would likely suspect soon if they did not already. It had been months since she and Calderon had been together. Her child would be half-elven, half-human. Would the baby have Dorric's auburn hair and green eyes? His wide, bright smile?

No. She had to set aside these romantic notions. A ritual had been passed down through the generations, a way to beseech the gods to find a new home for a child growing within. Emelyee allowed herself three days to nurture the child, and then she would return it to the heavens.

As the sun rose on the third day, it tinged the sky a peony pink, streaked with darker shades of rose and red. Emelyee knelt on the rug at the foot of her bed, the plush fibers cushioning her knees and feet. A wave of nausea swept over her, and she wrapped her arms around her abdomen, begging for a few more moments of stillness. Her time with the child was nearly spent.

Tears fell onto the patterned fabric. After this, she would have nothing left of her one experience of true love. She would relegate to the past everything she and Dorric had shared, a small monument to happiness that she could glance back upon, a few short weeks of which her grandmother would have been proud. A person couldn't endure such prolonged heaviness of heart, consumed by doubt and regret. She would find a way, somehow, to put Dorric behind her and earn Calderon's love and forgiveness. She had to find a way to forget.

Emelyee's stomach calmed. She closed her eyes, imagining the elf's arms wrapped around her shoulders, his delight at the news that they would have a child together. His final words had been a promise to think of her always. Could she spurn that love so quickly?

In their brief time together, she had never confessed to him what she felt. His eyes glittered when he said that he loved her, and she had offered only a kiss in return.

A voice whispered inside her, *Let this be your sign, cher'a*. Her grandmother's nickname for her, picked up on her nan's adventures through the Caldaran wilds. This child could be her answer to Dorric, a reciprocation of the amulet he'd left in her care. Though they would be forever apart, this child would keep him close through the years ahead.

EMELYEE ROSE FROM HER PRAYER POSITION, THANKING THE gods for the child she and Dorric would share rather than requesting that the gift be passed along. Carefully, she packed away her belongings. She would return to Aurora, where she would be free from her mother's urgings to reconsider and from Calderon's rage.

She sent for Reece that afternoon and asked that he prepare for their departure. They would stay at the house by the sea, so she would only need him and a few others to accompany her.

Emelyee knocked on Calderon's office door, and he called her inside. "I was not expecting you." He glanced up from the papers on his desk, quill poised over the family ledger.

"I only need a moment," Emelyee said.

He nodded, waiting.

"I am returning to Aurora," she began. Emelyee held up a finger to stop his reproach. "For my health and that of my child."

Calderon waved the declaration aside. "Bruden is well and will benefit from more time in the castle, learning what it means to be at court. And your color has returned. I see no need for this extravagance—" He froze, staring at her hand, which rested beneath her navel.

"For my health and the health of my new child, Calderon. I think it best if we return to a quiet life by the sea."

Her husband's eyes compressed to glimmering coals. "You . . . why . . . I won't allow it," he growled.

"It's not your decision."

Calderon flew to his feet and banged his fist on his desk. "You'll not bring a bastard into this castle!"

Emelyee clasped her hands together to prevent their shaking. She'd heard his outbursts often enough during their years together, but they'd rarely been directed at her before the last several days. "The Amastacia name is mine, Calderon, not yours to bestow," she said softly. "I will choose whether or not my child bears it."

He stared at her, mouth agape, as she turned and left the office, fingers clenched against her palms.

Emelyee sighed and leaned against the wall once she was safely outside her husband's quarters. Her pulse thumped in her chest, adrenaline flooding her body. Once she had calmed enough to proceed, she returned to the common area where Reece awaited her. Bruden and his nursemaid would join them soon. She left a note for her parents informing them of her decision and of her wish to be left in peace. The steward carried her remaining bags down to the waiting carriage, and they set off for Aurora.

The first week was consumed with dusting, organizing, and unpacking, but soon enough, Emelyee settled into a new routine of strolls along the beach and afternoons spent in the library. She filled the shelves of the large room with all of her favorite tales and Dorric's recommendations as well. Her second week, a letter arrived saying that Calderon was determined to stay away, and her mother's condition had worsened. Emelyee dismissed it, sure that her mother would fare better with time. She took Dorric's amulet from its box and wore it during her pregnancy, wishing the father's presence to keep her and the child company.

SEVERAL MONTHS LATER, EMELYEE HELD HER HALF-ELVEN BABY girl in her arms for the first time. Her breath caught as she studied the child. Beneath the swirls of red hair and pale, silver-white skin, the same bright green eyes that continued to haunt her dreams stared back at her. "I'll never forget you," she whispered. The young noblewoman blinked back tears and bent down to kiss the top of her daughter's head.

She spent several days working out the name, choosing something unique for the inheritor of the matrilineal Amastacia line. Finally, she fixed upon it: Iellieth. The baby chuckled and grinned the first time she said it, green eyes sparkling with delight.

Shortly thereafter, Emelyee put Dorric's amulet away. She resolved that it was in the child's best interest to become accustomed to what it meant to be an Amastacia. Iellieth would have security in this way, and a cultured upbringing. The court would learn to accept her.

Dorric would have been delighted with the little girl's blend of their features and her tiny pointed ears. Emelyee treasured each moment doubly, knowing the girl's elven father would never learn of her existence. Calderon, she was certain, would see to that.

CHAPTER 9

RIDEL

The evening gloom clung to Ridel as she stalked through the hallways of the Aurora estate, her every sense alive to the slightest movement. The rooms and halls were empty. She had suspected as much. The noblewoman had sought refuge in the smaller house by the sea.

Tall wildflowers whispered against her legs and arms as she ran, crouched low, across the fields. Alessandra had been very particular. Ridel had to perform each part of her job perfectly, leaving no trace, for her to receive a position equal to Lucien's.

She didn't see the opportunity to enhance her allegiance to the dark goddess as a betrayal of her former master, though on this, she and the lich were unlikely to see eye to eye. Lucien had motives and schemes of his own. He would have replaced her after this mission regardless of its success, or used her as an excuse for delaying the goddess's will, effectively painting a target on her back. No, she would take these matters into her own hands.

Alessandra instructed her to leave no mark of her attack that could evince any form of divine intervention. The simplest method, Ridel concluded, was to kill everyone inside and torch the structures. The home had one cellar entrance and a front and side door. The blonde woman's bedroom windows opened onto the back of the house, surrounded by forest. She would have difficulty escaping through the woods, especially with a baby in hand.

Ridel signaled the two assassins she'd procured in Cyrinia. The ideal balance between brutal and malleable was difficult to find, but she had been both persuasive and persistent in her efforts.

Two poisoned darts, each expertly thrown, toppled the guards at the front door. The lush flower beds beside the house cushioned their fall. She and her aides would take care of them on the way out. No sense slowing progress for unconscious watchmen.

Her assassins checked the windows along the front of the house. They signaled that no one moved inside. Ridel crouched beside the door and motioned for them to follow her.

Moonlight bathed the home's interior, illuminating the receiving room and lounge. From what she'd seen in the orb, the noblewoman didn't keep a servant or guard active inside at night.

Her assassins crept in behind her, and Ridel motioned for them to fan out across the front three rooms. They stuck to the umbral stretches between beams of moonlight, poised to follow her down the left-hand hallway.

But something wasn't right. Ridel sniffed, unable to place the sharp, woody scent she'd caught on the air.

"It's juniper," a low female voice spoke into the darkness. "You cannot go any further."

Ridel spun toward the lounge where the voice originated.

A sepia-skinned fae stepped out of the shadows. She lowered her head and smiled.

The negata withdrew her curved blade from its sheath, the edge dripping with lovingly crafted poisons. "Yvayne, is it? He warned me about you." Ridel cursed inwardly. Lucien had claimed the fae was unaware of their schemes. She should have suspected the falsehood.

"I see that you're putting the pieces together," Yvayne observed, shaking her head. "We should be cautious with whom we trust." The fae shrugged. "But let us return to the matter at hand. You must leave."

Moonlight caught the dark blade in Ridel's hand. Killing the fae would undoubtedly secure her position with Alessandra. The two she'd brought with her could dispatch the woman and child while she dealt with the more exotic prey.

"Navich, go," she commanded. The assassin didn't make a sound as he left the wall to her right. A light breeze brushed across Ridel's cheek as he ran past.

"Not you either," Yvayne said. She twirled the fingers of her left hand, opening them upward as though she were tossing powder into the sky. A faint whisper, like a dagger leaving its sheath.

Thunk. Navich fell. He struck his head on the thick oak floors, and blood began to seep along the wood grains. A whoosh overhead, and ropes of vines seized Navich and dragged him into the air. He hung upside down, tied to the rafters, blood dripping onto the floor.

The druid raised an eyebrow. "The warning I gave extends to the one who sent you. Leave. Now."

"You've no idea who sent me," Ridel growled. She lowered her body and sprinted at the fae woman.

Yvayne disappeared in a flash of mist, and Ridel slid to a stop.

"Ataret, now," Ridel ordered.

Her second assassin cried out as, with a low groan, the floorboards swallowed him to his waist. He turned to her, eyes wide in panic. His face contorted in pain, and he opened his mouth to scream, but a vine whipped down from above and gagged him.

"Shh," Yvayne whispered from the opposite corner, "you'll wake the baby."

Ataret gurgled, and his eyes bulged before he slumped over, a blood-soaked, leafy tendril sprouting from the back of his neck.

In her training, Ridel had learned that when facing powerful spell-casters, one should eliminate them before they had a chance to make an attack. She hadn't taken this advice seriously at first. She'd grown up possessing magic and doubted that another's would be able to destroy her.

On their second job together, she watched the only friend she'd carried over from childhood writhe and melt into little more than a puddle of black blood.

Rather than asking her to surrender, the mage responsible asked if she might like to join him, or if she would prefer to die. This seemed like a deceptively simple question. "What is the catch?" she asked.

"I will live forever," he said. "Most die in my employ, but while they live, they do so more gloriously than average mortals can begin to imagine."

"I am far from average."

"That's why I killed your friend." He smiled.

Ridel agreed to work for Lucien from that day forward, learning from his deep stores of magic and knowledge how to expertly manipulate the world around her.

She dove over one of the sofas for cover and tightened her grip on her poisoned dagger. Ridel exhaled slowly, searching for Yvayne's magical pulse. *There.*

Ridel leapt up and flung the dagger at the druid.

Yvayne grunted as the blade struck true, just below her collarbone.

The poison would do its work in a matter of moments.

Navich's body tumbled to the floor, landing with a sharp crunch.

Like death itself, Ridel thought, she slithered out of the room and darted into the hallway. The wind hissed through the trees outside, and waves crashed as the tide began its slow creep toward the shore.

A board creaked behind her. How had Yvayne withstood the poison? Ridel whirled around and threw another dagger. It skimmed past the druid's bare throat, missing by a hair's breadth.

The lavender eyes flashed, and Yvayne disappeared once more.

Ridel turned and found her adversary between herself and her objective. "I tire of this," Ridel snarled.

"We're nearly done." That maddening smile, and then Yvayne clapped her hands together at her chest.

A shout of thunder and an explosion of light burst from the fae. The force struck Ridel and shoved her backward down the hall. She screamed as the skin and hair burnt off her face, blisters immediately rippling over the raw flesh.

Ridel sprang up and charged. The druid would pay.

A concentrated white beam blazed forth from Yvayne's hand. Ridel screamed as it punctured her abdomen as though she'd been impaled by a spear. She fell forward, and the beam held her aloft.

Ridel raised her head, squinting at Yvayne. Blood dribbled from the side of Ridel's lip; it sizzled as it struck the beam and evaporated. The druid's eyes glowed as she watched the life leak from Ridel's body.

"They remain under my protection," Yvayne said. "They will stay safe from harm." She twirled her wrist and pulled her fingers into a ball. The beam inside Ridel narrowed, focusing in a ray of light that sliced her body in half. Her charred remains fell to the floor.

YVAYNE

Yvayne walked down the hall to Emelyee's door. She eased it open, thankful she'd warded it with silence as well as a shield. Her own presence, let alone the invasion, would have been difficult to explain.

The blonde noblewoman slept soundly, but the child stirred. Yvayne tucked the sage-green blanket back around the baby's shoulder, hoping to resolve her distress. Large green eyes blinked up at her with a soft coo of curiosity.

"Hello, Iellieth," Yvayne murmured. "Sleep now." She traced a line down the child's forehead and nose. "Your time will come soon enough." She wriggled her fingers through the air, and the conjured breeze gently rocked her back to sleep.

Yvayne crept over to Emelyee's bureau and peeked inside the top drawer. Resting beside the silks and other fine fabrics sat a box she remembered helping to forge. "Add silver to the inlay," she had suggested, "for protection."

Now, Yvayne whispered to the amulet nestled inside: "Serve her well."

She cast her wards once more and stepped outside to greet the dawn.

AND THAT WAS ONLY THE BEGINNING.

Ready to find out what happens next?! As you may have guessed, the enchanted amulet plays a key role in the events to come! If you loved the magic and adventure of *Aurora*, your journey continues in *Buried Heroes*. In the next phase of our adventure Iellieth is trapped beneath Calderon's thumb and desperate to escape the arranged marriage he's forcing her into.

Luckily for Iellieth, Dorric's amulet has other plans.

Be ready for more druids, more magic, and dangers galore in the first novel in the *Age of Azuria* high fantasy series. **Get your copy today!**

A RUNAWAY NOBLEWOMAN.

A CURSED WARRIOR.

AND THE QUEST TO SAVE THEIR WORLD.

Buried Heroes is an epic fantasy adventure filled with magic and destiny with a slow-burn romance subplot.

Step into a world of forgotten kingdoms, ancient relics, and a prophecy that will change everything. If you love found family, reluctant heroes, and forbidden magic, then continue your fantasy adventure with Buried Heroes today!

CURIOUS TO SEE WHAT HAPPENS BETWEEN IELLIETH AND TEODRIC AS THEY GROW UP?

It's true that *Buried Heroes* explores the beginning of Iellieth's epic quest, but that's only one way of looking at how her adventure begins.

Within the court of Linolynn, Calderon Amastacia has succeeded in expanding his power, and he's determined to get rid of his half-elven stepdaughter, no matter what.

But right under Calderon's nose, friendship blossoms into something more. Frederick and Aurelia's son Teodric sticks close by Iellieth's side. He wants to help her escape the cruel fate her stepfather is forcing her into.

Though he can scarcely admit as much to himself, Teodric wants something else besides—her heart.

In *Song of Parting*, Iellieth and Teodric are nearly grown and fighting to set their own way in the world. **Dive into their adventure today!**

WHAT IF SOMEONE LIKE RIDEL WAS THE HEROINE OF THE STORY?

Lucien isn't involved in this hypothetical scenario, but there *is* a dark romantasy with a stabby heroine and a morally gray hero waiting just for you!

HIS ENEMY'S COURTESAN. HER ONLY CHANCE OF ESCAPE.

Lord Silas Graveston's world is one of order, where honor ranks above all. But when his family's stolen necklace resurfaces at the throat of his enemy's new courtesan, Natalya Slipshayde, his calm facade cracks.

The closer Silas gets to her, the more he questions which trophy he most desires to yank from his rival's grasp: the necklace or Natalya.

Dive into the back-stabbing court of Draykemire today for an unforgettable dark fantasy adventure with secret identities, star-crossed lovers, and an incomplete prophecy.

routes… Until her elven father's amulet whisks her off to a frozen mountainside and the ancient warrior waiting to be awakened within.

Fate binds Iellieth and Marcon Colabra together, just as a magical curse binds Marcon to her amulet. Being trapped together isn't enough, as the forgotten warrior isn't the only dormant force awakening to this new world.

A fallen guardian hunts Iellieth—he knows she's the only one who can save Azuria from his dark mistress's plots, and he doesn't mean to be thwarted again.

Standing between Iellieth and the powerful mage, a young saudad woman fends off the press of werewolves teeming within the Caldaran forests. Persephonie Arelle and her people await the chosen one, promised long ago.

Across the Infinite Ocean, the bard-turned-pirate Teodric Adhemar faces a choice—submit to the atrocities ordered by his cruel admiral or surrender his mother's safety. The decision itself isn't difficult. It's living with the nightmares afterward.

In the northern wilds, a druid conclave serves as one of the last bastions of resistance against the aggressive press of the empire of Andel-ce Hevra. What they don't know is that the city has already made its fatal move against them. An attack is coming, and the magic of Genevieve Vendanges is unequal to the task of protecting her home.

Briseras Ravisthinia is without a home to protect, on the run from the empire and torn between two impossible quests— find the missing druid Fhaona or return to her cursed homeland and exact her revenge upon those who bound her into their service.

A reluctant pirate, an unpromising druid, a renegade huntress, and a magically inclined traveler stand between the forces of darkness that would destroy their world.

Uniting them all, a runaway noblewoman faces her destiny —she and she alone can save Azuria. If she fails herself, she fails them all.

For fans of magical quests, found family, and destiny driven heroes. Continue your adventure today!

JOURNEY DEEPER INTO AZURIA

For character art reveals, fantasy map deep-dives, and all the latest happenings in Azuria, visit bethballbooks.com/join to be part of my newsletter community, the Circle of Story.

If you'd like to support my work and get early access to bonus scenes, visit patreon.com/bethball.

And finally, for special editions and exclusive covers, visit bethballbooks.shop.

ABOUT THE AUTHOR

Beth Ball is a weaver of words and worlds spinning stories of druidic magic and the power of nature that span the epic fantasy realms of Azuria and Eldura. If you enjoy lyrical tales of action and adventure, dragons, werewolves, fae, wily foxes, and more, then grab your enchanted amulet, flaming longsword, poisoned dagger, or other mystical accessory of choice, and let's start our adventure!

You can find more of Beth's work and the legends of Azuria and Eldura at bethballbooks.com. And if you're looking for playable, immersive adventures in Azuria, visit groveguardianpress.com.

GLOSSARY

WORLDS & PLANES

Planes of Life, *three interconnected planes*, Azuria, Shadowlands, and Brightlands
Negative Planes, origin planes of the negata
Elemental Planes, one for each element, ruled over by and encompassing the power of each elemental titan
Astralei, spirit plane
Eldura, the name for the world in Azuria's ancient past before the Great Flood

DEITIES

Alessandra, "the dark goddess," goddess of negation
Cassandra, goddess of fate, patron deity of the saudad

FOLKLORIC HEROES

Hugh & Lilia, a Lycan and a fae, respectively; heroes before the Fall of the First Age who sacrificed their love to save their peoples
Daughters of Verdigris, Evelyn (creator of the lummenfae [Shadowlands fae], mother of Ravenna, and grandmother of Yvayne), Enid (creator of the brightfae [Brightlands fae] and mother of Lilia), and Lyric (creator of druids whose magic transferred to the prime plane)

PEOPLES OF AZURIA

Druids, mages and those bound to the earth, live in conclaves
Negata, people-group originating in the Negative Planes, most often distinguished by their horns
Saudad, storytellers and travelers blessed by the goddess Cassandra

ACKNOWLEDGMENTS

My special thanks to the wonderful friends, professionals, and mentors who have made this project and my author journey possible.

First, to Kristen, my incredible editor—thank you for seeing my work for what it could be and not just for the rough draft that it was. You encouraged me to write the book I *wanted* to write, and not simply what I could have managed at the time. For that, I am forever grateful.

And to Jonathan, my partner, best friend, and first reader. Thank you for staying in Azuria with me.

Finally, my special thanks to you, dear reader. I hope you've enjoyed this story, and I look forward to spending more time in Azuria with you.